ELMER and BUTTERFLY

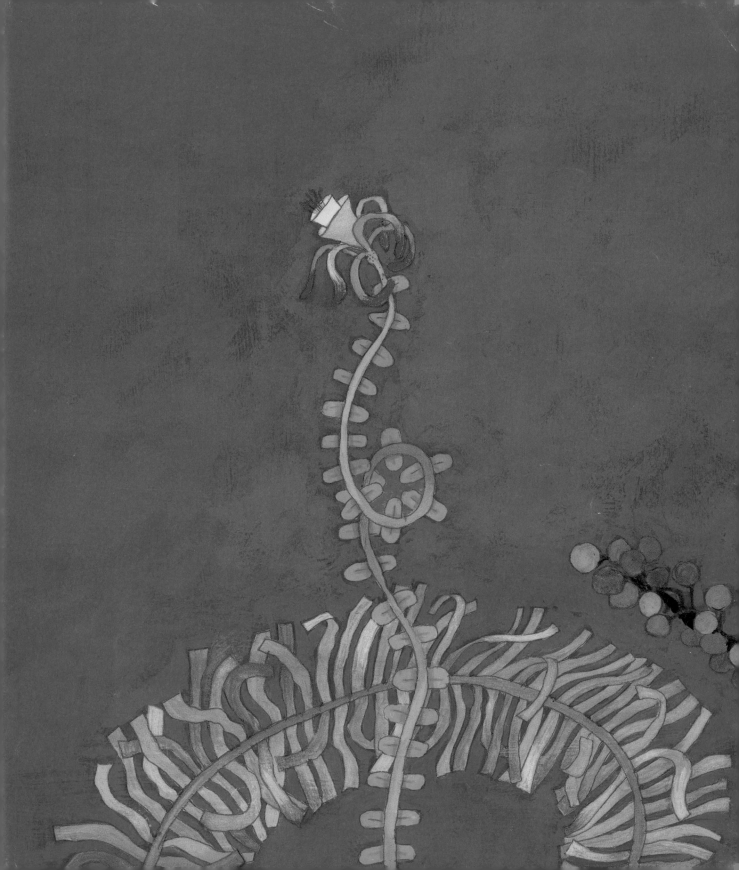

for Princess Bakhta

ELMER AND BUTTERFLY
A RED FOX BOOK 0 09 943968 9

First published in Great Britain by Andersen Press Ltd

Andersen Press edition published 2002
Red Fox edition published 2003

3 5 7 9 10 8 6 4 2

Copyright © David McKee, 2002

Red Fox Books are published by Random House Children's Books,
61–63 Uxbridge Road, London W5 5SA,
a division of The Random House Group Ltd,
in Australia by Random House Australia (Pty) Ltd,
20 Alfred Street, Milsons Point, Sydney, NSW 2061, Australia,
in New Zealand by Random House New Zealand Ltd,
18 Poland Road, Glenfield, Auckland 10, New Zealand,
and in South Africa by Random House (Pty) Ltd,
Endulini, 5A Jubilee Road, Parktown 2193, South Africa

THE RANDOM HOUSE GROUP Limited Reg. No. 954009
www.kidsatrandomhouse.co.uk

A CIP catalogue record for this book is available from the British Library.

Printed in Singapore

ELMER and BUTTERFLY

David McKee

RED FOX

Elmer, the patchwork elephant, was out walking when a shout came from up a tree: "Hello, Elmer."

"Is that you, Monkey?" Elmer called back.

"No, it's me," laughed cousin Wilbur from behind a bush.

"Hello, Wilbur," chuckled Elmer. "You are clever with your voice tricks. I'm going for a walk. See you later."

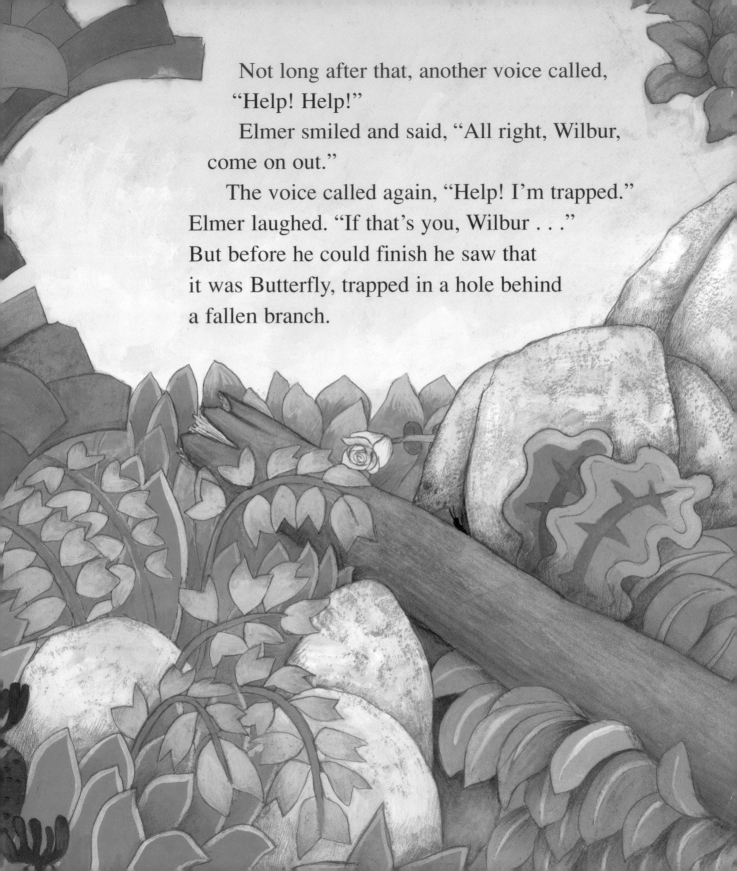

Not long after that, another voice called,
"Help! Help!"

Elmer smiled and said, "All right, Wilbur,
come on out."

The voice called again, "Help! I'm trapped."
Elmer laughed. "If that's you, Wilbur . . ."
But before he could finish he saw that
it was Butterfly, trapped in a hole behind
a fallen branch.

"Poor Butterfly," said Elmer and he lifted the branch to release her.

"Thank you, Elmer. The branch fell while I was in the hole," said Butterfly. "Perhaps one day I'll be able to repay you."

"Don't even think about it, Butterfly," said Elmer.

"If you do need me, just call my name," said Butterfly. "Wherever I am, I shall hear you."

"A butterfly saving an elephant, that's a good one!"
chuckled Elmer as he continued his walk.

At that point, a narrow path lead off the main one.

"I've never been here before," he said.

"This looks interesting."

The path suddenly lead out of the trees and along a cliff face
high above the valley below.

"This is dangerous," said Elmer. "And the path only goes to a cave.
I'll back back . . . Oh, dear! Going backwards here isn't easy.
I'll go to the cave, turn around and walk back normally."

Elmer was nearly there when the path started falling.
He rushed into the cave and peeped out. Part of the path had gone.
"Oh no!" he said. "There's no way back. Help!" he shouted.
There was no answer.

"Help!" Elmer called again. Still no answer.

"They're all too far away," he thought. "I'll try Butterfly.
Butterfly! Help!" he called.

He was about to try again when Butterfly arrived.

"Oh, Butterfly, thank goodness!" said Elmer.
"Now it's me who is trapped in a hole by the path
that has fallen."

"Don't worry, Elmer," said Butterfly.
"I'll get help."

Wilbur was amusing a group of elephants when Butterfly arrived. She quickly told them about Elmer. In no time the elephants were rushing to the rescue.

At the cliff top the elephants saw how dangerous it was and most kept away from the edge. Wilbur disappeared back among the trees.

One or two elephants carefully peeped over the edge
to try and spot Elmer. "I see his trunk," said one.

Wilbur soon came hurrying back, pulling a
very long, very strong creeper. He threw one
end over the edge of the cliff and called down,
"Catch hold, Elmer."

"Tie the creeper around you and hold on
tightly," said Butterfly. "Don't worry.
It will be all right."

Elmer tied the creeper firmly and called out, "I'm ready."

The elephants caught hold of the creeper and pulled. Elmer swung out from the cave and then upwards.

Once he was safe, Elmer thanked them all,
especially Butterfly.

"Fancy a butterfly saving an elephant," he said.

Then a shout came from the cave, "Don't forget me."

The elephants stared. "Who else is there?" said one.

"Just Wilbur's voice," laughed Elmer. "Let's tickle him."

But Wilbur was already running home.